First published in Great Britain 1987 by Beehive Books,
an imprint of Macdonald & Co. (Publishers) Ltd.
Greater London House, Hampstead Road, London NW1 7QX
A BPCC plc company
Text © 1987 by Macdonald & Co. (Publishers) Ltd
Illustrations © 1987 by Casterman, Tournai
Originally published in French under the title
AGLAE LA PETITE ABEILLE AU PAYS DES CHIFFRES
Published pursuant to agreement with Casterman, Paris

Printed in Belgium by Casterman, Tournai

BRITISH LIBRARY CATALOGUING IN PUBLICATION DATA

Hayes, Barbara
    Buzzy Bee in the land of numbers. (Buzzy Bee adventure books)
    I. Title   II. Deru, Myriam   III. Series
    813,.54   [J]   PZ7

ISBN 0-356-13484-9

BUZZY BEE

in

the Land of Numbers

Retold by Barbara Hayes
from an original story by Paule Alen
Illustrated by Myriam Deru

Beehive Books

One day, Buzzy Bee discovered
some buried treasure.
"Put it safely away in this
woolly bag," advised Buzzy's
friend, the ant.
"Certainly not!" replied Buzzy.
"I am going to spend it."

Buzzy flew to the market stall
which belonged to Sally Spider.
"Sally spins such beautiful,
silver lace," smiled Buzzy.
"I know she will sell me
something pretty."
In return for one silver
coin, Buzzy bought 1 lovely,
lace scarf.

Buzzy was very pleased
with the scarf and flew to visit
Tessa and Tommy Tortoise.
"If you give me that scarf and
a silver coin, you may take 2 of
our delicious strawberries,"
said Tommy.

Buzzy loved strawberries and
gave the scarf and the coin
to Tommy Tortoise.
Next, Buzzy met three donkeys
who were flying toy aeroplanes.
The donkeys liked strawberries.
"You may have 3 aeroplanes if
you give us those two ripe
strawberries and one silver
coin," they told Buzzy.

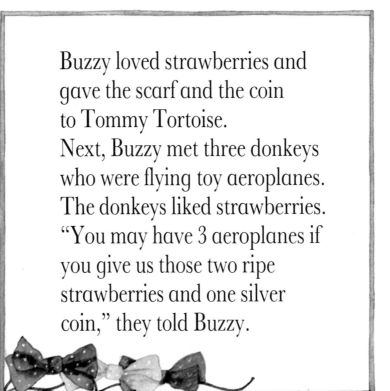

Buzzy Bee agreed and
flew the three aeroplanes
right over the rainbow.
And there, sliding down
the rainbow, Buzzy met
four little bees with 4 jars
of the best honey.
Buzzy gave them the
aeroplanes and a coin and
took the honey away.

"Honey will do me good,"
smiled Buzzy, taking the honey
into the forest. Suddenly,
five bear cubs came along.
"You must give us a coin and
all the honey in exchange for
these 5 balloons," growled
the bear cubs.
"Of course!" gulped Buzzy.
"Take it at once!"

Buzzy clutched the balloons
and flew high into the sky.
Then six seagulls came cawing
and flapping around the bright
balloons.
"We will give you 6 feathers for one
coin and those five balloons,"
they screeched. "Is that a
bargain or are you looking for
some trouble?"

"It is a very good bargain,"
agreed Buzzy nervously, who
did not really like feathers.
"We think those six feathers
are beautiful!" called seven
Indians. "Give them to us
with a silver coin and we will
give you 7 necklaces."

The necklaces were much too heavy for Buzzy to carry. Then Buzzy remembered Mrs Mouse who lived nearby. Mrs Mouse had seven little mice and they were all having a birthday party. So Buzzy gave the mice the seven necklaces and the mice gave Buzzy 8 iced cakes.

"Now I am happy at last,"
smiled Buzzy, settling in a
field to eat the eight
iced cakes.
"If you give us a silver
coin and those eight cakes
you may have these 9 pairs
of socks we have knitted,"
said nine sheep in the field.
So, Buzzy had to agree.

"Oh dear!" sighed Buzzy trying
to bundle together the nine
pairs of socks. "I have only
one coin left of my treasure
and I have lost my way home."
"Give me the last coin and the
socks," squeaked a centipede,
"and I will give you these
10 magic arrows which will
show you the way home."

"Thank you," said Buzzy and
followed the arrows home.
"I have had a good day,"
Buzzy thought. "I have bought
1 scarf, 2 strawberries,
3 aeroplanes, 4 jars of honey,
5 balloons, 6 feathers,
7 necklaces, 8 cakes, 9 pairs
of socks and 10 magic arrows
that brought me back home."

1 0 6 4 3 7 2 1 6 2 8 5 9 1